Cop Cat rode his mule
up the road.
Cop Cat had a rope
on The Kid.

Cop Cat had to take
The Kid to jail.

His mule sat in the road.
"Get up," said Cop Cat.
But the mule did not
get up.

"Get up!" said Cop Cat
to the mule.
Cop Cat gave his bit
a tug.

But the mule did not
get up.
The mule sat in the
road.

The mail dog rode up
the road to Cop Cat.
The mail dog had the
mail.

"Wait," said Cop Cat.
But the mail dog did
not wait.
The mail dog rode on.

The mule ate the oats,
but he did not get up.

As Cop Cat fed the
mule, The Kid ran.
"Wait!" said Cop Cat.

But The Kid did not wait.
He ran in the rain.
The Kid did not want to
go to jail.

The mule got up.
He ran to get The Kid.

Cop Cat ran up the
road to get The Kid.
Cop Cat was a sad cat.
He was wet.

Cop Cat came to
the mule.
The mule was on
The Kid.

The mule did wait, and
he made The Kid wait.
Cop Cat tied his rope
to The Kid.

Cop Cat and his mule
rode on to the jail.
"I am a fine cop,"
said Cop Cat.